THE KING OF
Skittledeedoo

"Light tomorrow with today."
Elizabeth Barrett Browning

For all my family and friends — you are all "jewels" in my tiara.
Patricia Rust

MARKOWITZ PUBLISHING
ISBN 0-9655890-6-4 LCCN 98-067685
Printed in China

*O*nce upon a time in the land of Skittledeedoo
Lived a kingdom of kind folks and kingly ones, too.

There were short folks and tall folks and twin folks of two;
There were old folks and young folks and dogs of bright blue.

The king ruled the castle and everyone there;
Dressed in robes of silk and velvet, he hadn't a care.

His valet groomed the king for his crown everyday
He picked out his robes and made sure they would stay.

With brooches and big gemstones that shone in the sun,
The king felt it was his duty to be admired by everyone.

His crown was so large; it was really quite grand.
His crown was so big that it could be seen throughout
the land!

Each day the king would stroll from place
to place
Glistening gold in his kingdom,
putting a smile on every face.

Life was good and life was full;
For a king, preening and prancing
were never dull.

Then one day tragedy struck
 A fire broke out and the town folk ran amuck!

Skittledeedoo was a fiefdom now marred
No longer a kingdom; it was more than just charred.

The castle burned all the way down to the earth,
And the king ran out displaying all of his girth.

6

He wore only a towel round his round as round waist
It was all he could find in the fiery haste

"Oh my, what will my people all think?!"
Cried the king as he ran out into the streets.

8

But no one paid him any attention at all.
They never noticed him in his towel, they didn't notice him at all.

"Calm, kingdom, calm yourselves, people I beseech you listen to me!
I am your king of our kingdom near the sea.

Don't shout! It is Skittledeedoo that belongs to you
I am here to help though I know not what to do!"

9

You are not our king!" exploded the crowd.
"Where is your crown and your rings of which
you are proud?"

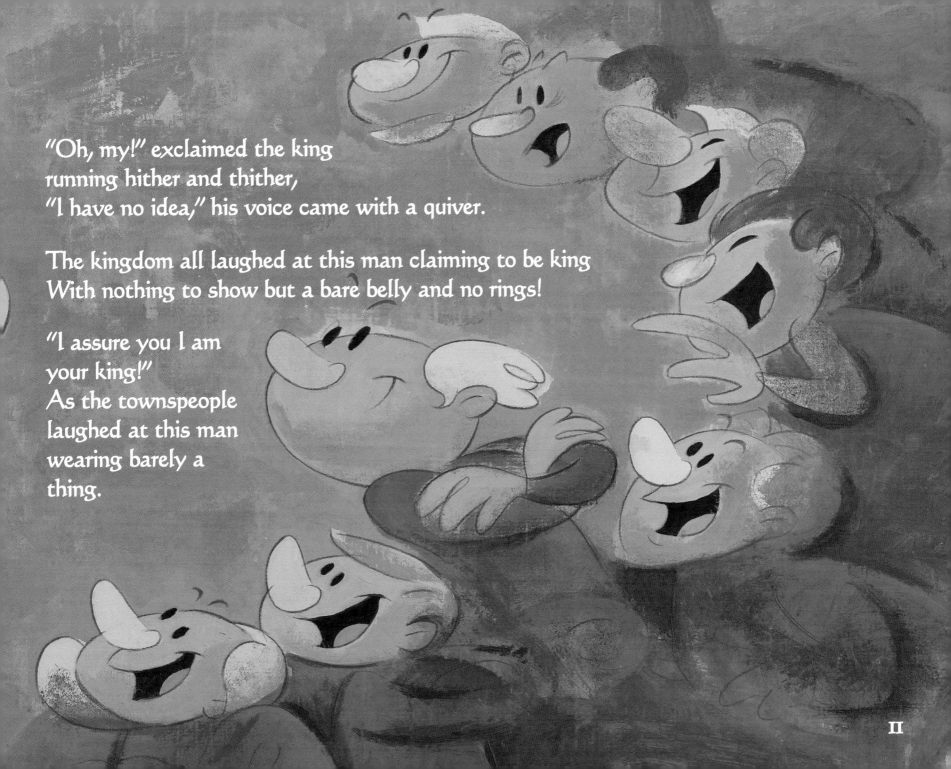

"Oh, my!" exclaimed the king
running hither and thither,
"I have no idea," his voice came with a quiver.

The kingdom all laughed at this man claiming to be king
With nothing to show but a bare belly and no rings!

"I assure you I am
your king!"
As the townspeople
laughed at this man
wearing barely a
thing.

"If you are our king, prove it, kind king.
Then for you we will do most anything."

The king scratched his bald head which matched his bald belly.
How could he think; his mind had turned to jelly!

"Ask me anything you would ask a king!
Ask me about jade and rubies and things!"

"What is two plus two?" came a question from a boy, not shy.
"Why I can answer that! Five!" came the king's robust reply.

The little boy snickered and all the town laughed.
"With an answer like that, he might be the court jester
who's daft!"

"I am your king!" said the king as he hoisted up his towel.
"This questioning is unfair. I am too nervous and am forced to cry foul."

"Okay," said a member of the crowd, each expecting to hear "four".
As another announced, "We have no choice but to ask of you more."

The king paced and thought with diligence and glee,
"As your king, I'll answer any questions you ask of me."

The king sat down on a big rock blackened and hard
Not exactly a throne but a perch, which too had been charred.

"I am as ready as a king will ever be
    Without his royal valet and his royal crown and jewelry."

"Spell potatoes, kind king, if that's who you are.
If you spell it correctly, we will know you near and far."

"Potatoes?" asked the king, "It's as easy as
one, two, four.
P-O-T-A-T-O-W-S.
Bring on some more."

16

The crowd was all laughing, forgetting the fire,
Why surely this was the king's jester there to prevent ire!

A little boy faced the king eye to eye,
"Are you ready, sire? I've a question to ply."

"Aye," came the king's determined reply.
And with that he looked the lad straight in the eye.

17

"How would a king spell the cherished word 'mother'?
Clearly, this is an important word and like no other."

The king would have stroked his beard; but he had not a beard to stroke.
He just shook his head and answered the young bloke.

"M - U - T - H - E - R" would seem right to me.
Yes, I am sure that's how a king would spell mother mightily."

HER

The little boy who had tried to show his respect
Couldn't help but completely crack up as the answer was absolutely incorrect!

He laughed as hard as the whole town of Skittledeedoo
He laughed as hard as if one plus nine equaled two.

19

The king look perplexed, not understanding
the laughter one bit.
He started to grow angry and throw a kingly fit!

"Look here. I said I was your king and
I mean it by gosh!
Devoted to my kingdom, not all
this questioning mish mosh . . ."

"If you are our king of Skittledeedoo,
then surely you can spell that word, too."

A girl curtseyed very politely as she made
this request
To the king wearing the towel, which
was all he had left.

"Skittledeedoo, well I can say it of course.
It's such a simple kingdom name, why it could be spelled by my horse!

S - C - l - Diddle - D- Dee- Doo.
With all your questions, you have me quite confused."

The poor king heaved a heavy sigh.
Then his sigh turned into a big kingly cry.

"I am your king. I just cannot add, write, or spell.
Have I treated you unjustly? Have I not treated you well?"

All the crowd agreed that they loved their dear king,
But this was not their king – a king who could not spell nor count
nor read could be no such thing!

The little boy and mannered girl both liked the king very much;
And were terribly sad that the king had flunked this test in the clutch.

"We shall teach you to spell. And to learn very well.
Even if you are not our king, on these things you must dwell."

So, the king was invited to go to school every day
And he went and learned his lessons without delay.

A scrap of nice fabric would blow by him now and again,
The king would grab it up when he put down his pen.

Soon he had enough fabric for a colorful cloak
And by and by he fashioned a crown from a branch of old oak.

The teacher kept teaching the king with a touch that was light,
She even taught him how to spell the word "kingdom" just right.

Then, the king stood, now looking quite regal.
With the stately look of a big kingly bald eagle.

"I am your king. I reclaim my throne."
And, as dawn came, on his oak crown, the sun softly shone.

The crowds, they bowed and scraped very low,
"Of course he is our king; he is dressed just so."

By now the king held court from his place on the rock;
Learning much from the children, like how to spell "sock."

The kingdom was happy to have now a king;
Just as happy as the king was to learn everything!

The little boy was most noble indeed
As he continued to teach the vain king to learn and to read.

The king promised the boy fancy jewelry and a gold bell,
But the boy turned him down and said,
"Let's just learn to read and spell."

"S - T - E - E - D," tried the king, "This surely is steed."
"Very good," said the boy, "Very good indeed."

And with that, from out of nowhere, the king's horse galloped over the ground.
Bearing the king's true crown which after the fire the steed had found.

The king turned and gave the boy his king's crown,
"This is now yours. It weighs in at 2 pounds."

"Thank you, your majesty, but I have but one request.
Please spell Skittledeedoo; then we can take a much needed rest."

"Skittledeedoo is a breeze to do," smiled the king as he began,
"S - K - I -T -T - L - E - D - E - E - D - O - O,"
through the letters he ran.

"Skittledeedoo burned to the ground
but soon we will all be found
Living on the rebuilt castle grounds!

Two miles high and four miles wide
All of Skittledeedoo shall live inside."

"And all I decree, all that I say,
Is that I want to learn one new thing every single day."

The End